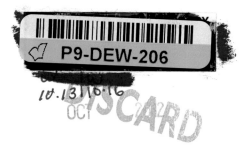

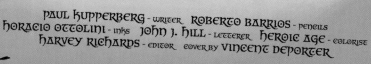

DARKNESS FALLS ON
SCOOBY-DOO!

PROPERTY OF C L P !

THE BLACK KATZ

PAUL KUPPERBERG - WRITER ROBERTO BARRIOS - PENCILS
HORACIO OTTOLINI - INKS JOHN J. HILL - LETTERER HEROIC AGE - COLORIST
HARVEY RICHARDS - EDITOR COVER BY VINCENT DEPORTER

Spotlight

visit us at www.abdopublishing.com

Reinforced library bound edition published in 2012 by Spotlight, a division of the ABDO Group, 8000 West 78th Street, Edina, Minnesota 55439. Spotlight produces high-quality reinforced library bound editions for schools and libraries. Published by agreement with Warner Bros.—A Time Warner Company. The stories, characters, and incidents mentioned are entirely fictional. All rights reserved. Used under authorization.

Printed in the United States of America, Melrose Park, Illinois.
052011
092011
This book contains at least 10% recycled materials.

Library of Congress Cataloging-in-Publication Data

Kupperberg, Paul.
 Scooby-Doo and the black Katz / writer, Paul Kupperberg ;
penciller, Roberto Barrios. -- Reinforced library bound ed.
    p. cm. -- (Scooby-Doo graphic novels)
 ISBN 978-1-59961-915-6
1. Graphic novels. I. Scooby-Doo (Television program) II. Title.
III. Title: Scooby-Doo and the black cats.
 PZ7.7.K87Sb 2011
 741.5'973--dc22
                                 2011001223

All Spotlight books are reinforced library bindings
and manufactured in the United States of America.

SCOOBY-DOO!
Table of Contents

MAYBE BECAUSE HE'D LOSE *ACCESS* TO THE CHECKBOOK...?

HE *DID* SEEM QUICK TO GIVE MONEY TO STRANGERS.

SNIF.. SNIF...

HE CAN'T JUST, LIKE, HAND OUT CASH FOR *NO* REASON.

HE HAS A REASON...*CAT* DAMAGE!

WE NEED TO TALK TO SOMEBODY WHO *ISN'T* COMPLETELY CAT-CRAZY. I SAY WE START...

"...WITH THE LOCAL NEWSPAPER!"

⸫GROAN!⸫ NOT THOSE STUPID CATS...

DON'T BE A DANGED *FOOL.* CATS CAN'T CAUSE BAD LUCK...

...BUT SOME PEOPLE BELIEVE *ANYTHING!* LOST YOUR KEYS? DIDN'T GET PROMOTED? TRIPPED AND BROKE YOUR LEG? *BLAME* THE BLACK CATS!

...*AGAIN!* EVER SINCE MRS. KATZ WENT TO THE BIG LITTER BOX IN THE SKY, THAT'S *ALL* I HEAR ABOUT!

SO ARE THEY, LIKE, *REALLY* CAUSING PEOPLE TO HAVE BAD LUCK, MR. BELLOWS?

DUMBEST THING I EVER HEARD! TOWN'S SO RILED UP, THEY'RE TRYING TO PASS A LAW *BANNING* THE CATS FROM KATZBURG.

HOW THE DEVIL DO YOU BAN CATS?!

ER... WHOSE IDEA WAS *THAT*, MR. BELLOWS?

SNIF.. SNIF..